WITCH HOUSE

We stood there watching for another five minutes or so until the flames had eaten through the piled-up junk and there was barely anything left.

"I wonder how it started?" Jenna asked.

I yawned and was just about to say that I hadn't the faintest when outside the big black cat strode into view. For a moment its bulky shape was silhouetted on the glowing embers of the bonfire, where it threw a long, wavering shadow, then it disappeared into the darkness again.

"How did it start?" I said. "There's your answer. Bet that cat and its owner had something to do with this. . ."

Look out for:

Haunted House
Plague House
Horror House

WITCH HOUSE

MARY HOOPER

SCHOLASTIC

Scholastic Children's Books,
Commonwealth House, 1–19 New Oxford Street,
London, WC1A 1NU, UK
A division of Scholastic Ltd
London ~ New York ~ Toronto ~ Sydney ~ Auckland
Mexico City ~ New Delhi ~ Hong Kong

First published in the UK by Scholastic Ltd, 2005

Copyright © Mary Hooper, 2005

ISBN 0 439 95888 1

Printed and bound by Nørhaven Paperback A/S, Denmark

10 9 8 7 6 5 4 3 2 1

The right of Mary Hooper to be identified
as the author of this work has been asserted by her in
accordance with the Copyright, Designs and Patents Act, 1988.

CHAPTER ONE

"Of course," said Ratty Ratcliffe, "there are no such things as witches."

I nudged Jenna and she nudged me back. We both believed in witches and also in ghosts, spooks and spectres – in fact, anything at all of the supernatural variety. Well, we'd certainly seen enough since we'd been living in Bensbury.

It was a dark and misty evening in the middle of October and everyone – practically the whole village – was gathered in Mrs Hugo's house to hear about a witch who'd lived in the village a few hundred years back. Miss Ratcliffe, known by Jenna and me as Ratty because of her pointy rodent nose and big front teeth, was in charge of proceedings and stood in front of the grand piano (yeah, it was that sort of house) sounding off to everyone. She knew all about what the village had been like in the olden days; ran some sort of historical society where they did nothing but talk about that stuff.

"I've called this meeting to talk about Old Ma Morgan, who lived and died four hundred years ago," she said, and there was a murmur of excitement as all the crinklies took this in. "According to the documents I've read, at first the villagers liked having a wise woman around. She'd make up herb potions and medicines to cure their ailments, and help them find things that were missing."

I pulled a face at Jenna. That wasn't what you wanted to hear about witches, was it? What you wanted to hear about was them flying on broomsticks, stirring up frogs in cauldrons and dancing with black imps – that sort of stuff.

"One year, however, the harvest failed," Ratty went on, "and the villagers turned against her. They said she was putting evil spells on people."

"Evil spells!" I said with relish. "That's more like it."

Ratty frowned at the interruption.

"What *sort* of spells?" I asked her. "You mean like people getting warts all over them?"

"If you let me continue, Jake, you may find out."

"OK," I said, because Mum, sitting behind me, was poking me in the back to be quiet.

"One villager reported that whenever he went out he was surrounded by a swarm of flies; he said that was because Old Ma Morgan had put a curse on him. Someone else said that their cat had died for no apparent reason, another said that his cows had started giving blue milk. . ."

"Cool!"

"Jake!" Mum hissed at me.

"Well, different coloured milk would be good, wouldn't it?" I said. "I wouldn't mind drinking blue milk. Or even green. You'd expect it to be green, actually, wouldn't you? What with all the grass they eat."

There was a heavy sigh from Ratty.

"What?" I said. "I'm just *saying*. . ."

It was one thing I knew about cows – that they ate a lot of grass. I didn't know much more about them because I hadn't been brought up in the boring old country, but in a proper place with shops and a cinema and skateboard parks. And a football pitch, natch. Here in Bensbury, me and

Jenna and Mum were living over the only shop, and there was nothing around but a heap of cottages with a load of old biddies living in them. In fact, the only thing which stopped Jenna and me from dropping dead of boredom was that we'd discovered that there were quite a few ghosts around. Real live (or dead, I suppose that should be) ghosts. Some were nice and friendly, like Wellington the phantom dog. Some weren't, like Sorrel, the girl in the mirror who'd tried to drag Jenna back into the seventeenth century.

"Shall I go on, Jake?" Ratty asked rather sarcastically.

"Yeah," I said. Because I wanted to know more about the witch, I really did.

"Thank you," said Ratty. "Well, soon anything bad that happened in the village was blamed on Old Ma Morgan and her strange black cat, which was said to be her familiar and so have the power to assume different shapes. Eventually the watchmen arrested Ma for witchcraft. She was tried, found guilty, then burned on a bonfire on the thirty-first of October, the eve of All Hallows. . ."

"Hallowe'en!" I put in quickly, in case anyone didn't know.

Ratty ignored me. "This year will be the four hundredth anniversary of the day the witch was burned, and it's been suggested that the village hold a pageant to mark the occasion. That's why I've asked everyone to Mrs Hugo's lovely home to discuss what form it will take. We want everyone to take part, from the oldest right down to our youngest, newest, villagers. . ."

Seeing as Jenna and I were the youngest by about a hundred years, every eye in the room there turned to look at us.

I scowled right back. If they thought I was going to dress up as a historical village boy wearing a smock and chewing a bit of straw, they were barking up the wrong tree. *Well* up the wrong tree. The only historical figure I'd dress up to be was Bobby Moore, captain of England, collecting the World Cup, 1966.

"Of course, the twins would be delighted to take part," Mum chipped in.

Dream on, I thought.

"They always take a great deal of interest in the goings-on in the village."

Only ghostly goings-on.

I felt, rather than heard, Jenna say this, because we sometimes know what the other is thinking.

At first I thought this was just something to do with being twins, but since we've been living here, other weird stuff has been happening. Like Jenna has gone a bit psychic and often sees and hears ghosts and stuff. Sometimes I do, too, but any messages I get are usually channelled through Jenna (and don't ask me how this works because I haven't got the faintest).

Mum was nudging us to say something. Because she runs the shop and post office, she's dead keen for us to be smarmily polite to everyone in the village. She reckons it will make them use the shop more.

"What sort of a part would I have?" Jenna asked.

"I don't know yet, dear," Ratty said, "Mrs Snape is casting the roles."

Everyone turned to look at Mrs Snape – known to me and Jenna as Snotty Snape because of the permanent drip quivering on the end of her nose.

"Well, Jenna, I thought you could be a village maiden," Snotty said. "A beautiful village maiden cursed by the witch."

"Oh, OK!" said my sister, beaming all over her face.

"What about me?" I asked. "Can I be some

sort of wicked male witch – a wizard – and put spells on people?"

"There was only one witch – Old Ma Morgan," Ratty put in, "and even she was actually a harmless old woman. Mrs Butley will be playing her."

All eyes now turned to Mrs Butley, known to us as Bumface Butley because she and her husband have got very round, pink faces. These names came from an idea Mum gave us. You think of a memorable nickname for someone which chimes with their real name and that helps you remember it: Mr Murray is a farmer with a stinking slurry yard; he's Slurry Murray. Mrs Scudder is all-over-the-place scatty so she's Scatty Scudder. Mr Green is always moaning; he's Grouchy Green.

"I was on the stage, you know," Bumface Butley said, and she simpered around at everyone. "They said my *Juliet* was quite exquisite."

"That must have been a few years back," I said, and heard a faint groan from Mum.

"Are you *sure* there wasn't a wizard?" I asked Ratty.

"Perfectly sure," she said. "There was a green man, as they were called, in the next village – in Grimbridge – but not here."

"Well, I could be the green man visiting you from Grimbridge," I said. "I'd wear a big cloak with mystical signs on and do tricks."

"Ha!" Mr Magic put in. "If there's a wizard to be played, I shall be he."

I scowled at him. Mr Magic, as he liked to be called (Mr Tragic, Jenna and I called him) was a "Celebrity Conjurer and Entertainer" who really fancied himself. He was forever getting eggs out of your ears or asking you to choose a card out of a pack, even when you'd made it clear that you thought he was a complete plonker.

"I'm afraid there will be *no* part for a wizard, green man, magician or whatever else you might call it," Ratty said firmly. She clapped her paws. "Now," she said, "I just want to cover the basic points of the pageant this evening, so we can all start to think about what we might do. Mr Starr and I have come up with a few basic ideas. Mr Starr, if you please. . ."

Stuffer Starr got up to speak. He's a funny-looking bloke, dead scruffy, with more grey hair coming out of his nose and ears than he's got on his head. We call him Stuffer, because he's a taxidermist. That is, he finds dead animals, stuffs them and puts them in glass cases. Pretty weird, eh? But actually, as Jenna and I had started saying, just NFB: Normal For Bensbury.

"We thought that we'd construct an exact copy of the witch's house just where it used to be, on the village green," said Stuffer. "I say house, but it's more like a hovel, really. Very basic. The play would be centred around this hovel, and we'd have stalls and sideshows as well."

"We've managed to find an etching of the real, original witch's house," Ratty added, pointing to a framed picture standing on the piano. "We thought we'd act out various scenes: first, show Old Ma Morgan dispensing her medicines to people; then have the village turning against her; finally, have a stylized re-enactment of the witch burning."

"Won't that be a bit dangerous?" someone asked.

"*Stylized*," Ratty repeated. "We wouldn't really set fire to her. We'd just tie her up and people would dance round her in an imitation of the flames. We'd hold the pageant on Hallowe'en and leave the actual lighting of the bonfire until November the fifth."

"What d'you think?" Jenna asked me in a whisper.

"Yawn," I said. I could have found better things to do on a Friday night.

We broke for refreshments, which was the main reason Mum had got me there. I'd thought, seeing as the meeting was at Mrs Huge-o's (Jenna and I called her this because she was) there would have been masses to eat, but it was just crisps, so I reckoned she'd eaten everything else before we'd arrived.

The lady herself, wearing a big brown dress which made her look like a tree trunk, caught me stuffing a mouthful of cheese-and-onion into my mouth. "Ah, young boy," she said. "I understand from your mother that you might be interested in doing a little job for me."

"Bllleeaaaaghhh," I said, outraged. Or I didn't actually *say* it, but this was the noise that the mouthful of crisps made.

"Quite. So she and I have agreed that you'll come and dig my garden over after school and on Saturdays."

"Beoughhh!" I protested.

"Good. That's settled, then. See you tomorrow at ten o'clock."

I looked at her departing back, gulped down

the rest of the crisps and went to find Mum. "Why did you say I'd dig Mrs Huge-o's garden?" I asked fiercely.

"Mrs *Hugo*," Mum corrected me.

"Whatever."

"Jake, you've been saying for ages that you want to earn some pocket money! Here's your chance."

"I don't want to *dig* for it," I said. Digging sounded too much like hard work. "Besides. . ."

"Besides what?"

"Jenna and I are usually busy doing stuff at weekends." Ghost-hunting sort of stuff, I meant, but I didn't want to actually say that in case she went off on one.

"Nothing important," Mum said. "A couple of hours' hard digging on a Saturday morning will do you good."

"Oh, right. You know that for a fact, do you?" I said, and was just going to develop this line further when I noticed that Jenna was standing by the piano holding the picture of the witch's house and looking a bit green around the chops. I went over to ask her what was up.

"Have a look at this," she said a bit shakily.

I looked. The picture showed the witch's house

standing in a clearing. It was rickety and ramshackle and looked just about big enough to have a bed and a chair and a fireplace inside. Tall trees stood behind it; there was a black cat sitting outside and a witch's broom leant against the planked wooden door.

"What do you see?" she asked, and when I shrugged and said nothing much, she told me to look at it again, and look *hard*.

I did so, and as I stared at the picture, really concentrated, I thought I saw the door of the hut blur and fade and a figure appear there: a hunched, ugly figure of a woman wearing a drab cloak. One arm was raised, shaking her fist; in the other she held a staff.

I gave a yelp and quickly shoved the picture back on the piano.

"Exactly," said Jenna. "I saw it, too."

We stared at each other, my heart pounding away as if I'd just fluffed an open goal in the last minute of the World Cup Final.

"The thing is," Jenna said earnestly, "Ratty said the witch was actually just a ordinary old woman who'd been picked on, but I don't think she was. I think – I *feel* – that she might have been a real witch."

I nodded, seized with a sudden, horrible fear. If Sorrel, the girl from the seventeenth century, could reach out to us through a mirror, then maybe this Old Ma Morgan could get to us through a picture.

But that was just crazy.

Wasn't it?

CHAPTER TWO

I was lying in bed the next morning, half asleep and half awake, trying *not* to think about that witch picture but instead concentrating on a really funny dream I'd had about Scotland winning the World Cup, when I heard Jenna talking to herself. She's a bit batty, my sister, so the fact that she was talking to herself wasn't strange in itself, and it wasn't until I heard, "You're a *lovely* cat, aren't you? What a big fine cat you are!" that I rolled out of bed and went to see what was going on. If there was a cat in the house, I knew Mum would go mad because she's allergic to them.

I pushed open the door of Jenna's room and saw the cat immediately, sitting on her duvet right on top of her. It was a black cat, but not sleek-and-shiny black, more like a big old saggy cushion, its fur all manky and its ears bitten.

"What's that thing?" I said to Jenna, and as I spoke the cat turned to stare at me. I thought that cats always had green eyes but *this* one's were hard and grey.

"It's a cat," said Jenna.

"Ha ha. Where did it come from?" I sniffed the air. "And I think the answer to that might be a dustbin."

"Sssh," Jenna said, "you'll hurt its feelings. It must have come in downstairs."

I frowned. "It couldn't have done. Mum would have seen it."

Jenna shrugged. "OK. It must have come through the window."

"Your window's closed," I pointed out. "So's mine. And even if they were open, how would a cat climb up a sheer brick wall?"

Jenna considered this. "Cats are quite clever," she said. "If they're cold and hungry and want to get into someone's house, they'll find a way."

I moved a bit closer to inspect the cat. "Is it real? I mean, it's not a *phantom* cat, is it?" This might have seemed like a silly thing to say but, seeing as ghost dogs aren't unknown in Bensbury, there was every chance this cat might not really be there.

"It's definitely not a ghost – it feels like a lead weight sitting on my tummy."

I gave another sniff. "And it smells like it needs a good bath."

"That's just a ... a sort of damp cat smell," Jenna said, and the cat turned to stare at me again with its steel-grey eyes, as if it knew I didn't like it.

A moment later Mum appeared on the landing. "Hurry up, you two!" she called through the open door. "I could do with some help in the shop, Jenna – and Mrs Hugo's expecting you, Jake."

As I turned to start making objections about Huge-o, Mum came in the room and saw the cat. "What's *that* doing here?" she said, and sneezed. "You know I'm allergic to them."

"It just appeared," said Jenna.

"Well, now it can disappear. Take it straight down, Jake, and show it the door."

I was about to object to this and say that the cat wasn't *my* responsibility, not being in *my* bedroom, but then realized I had something much more important to moan about. "I haven't really got to go to old Huge-o's today!" I protested.

"The sooner you go, the sooner you start earning money," said Mum. Then she sneezed, said, "Cat out!" and disappeared behind a welter of paper handkerchieves, waving to indicate that she wasn't going to enter any further discussion.

Groaning, I picked up the cat – it was as heavy as it looked – carried it downstairs and chucked it out. Once chucked, it sat on the doorstep and looked back at me balefully through the shop door, as if saying that it was going to get back in if it wanted to, so *there*. It was strange, I thought, that there had been a meeting the previous evening about a witch and her black cat, and now one had appeared out of nowhere. A bit spooky, that.

One large breakfast later I kicked my football across the green, winged it past the No Ball Games notice without a glance and headed for Mrs Huge-o's house. I'd tried – Beckham knows I'd tried – to get out of the Helping of the Huge-o, but Mum said that she'd *promised* I'd be there and I wasn't to let her down.

"Mrs Hugo's a good customer with a large capacity," she'd said.

"Is that a new word for bum?"

"A large *spending* capacity," Mum said severely. "She uses our post office and shop a lot and we don't want to get on the wrong side of her."

"No, it'd take too long to walk back," Jenna said, which I thought was quite funny, for her.

"Mrs Snape was saying that since Mrs Hugo's husband has been abroad, she's found the garden too much for her," Mum added. "That's why she wants you to dig it over."

Thinking about all this, I'd just broken into a run to retrieve my football when I heard a squeaky voice calling, "I say! I say, Jake!" and I looked over to see Mrs (Squeaker) Squires leaning over her hedge and waving to me.

"Did you squeak?" I asked.

"Yes, I did. Have you seen my cat anywhere?"

So it was hers, I thought. "Is it a big black one?"

"No, it's not," she squealed in her funny high voice. "It's small and tortoiseshell. Lovely markings and white paws. Answers to the name of Mittens."

I shook my head. "I haven't seen it. I've seen a huge black old cushion-cat, though. D'you know anyone that's lost one?"

But she wasn't interested in any other sort of cat. "Just look out for my Mittens, will you?" she said. "She hasn't been around since last night and I'm very worried."

I said I would and flicked up my ball to do keepy-uppies across the rest of the green. And then something odd happened: someone *else* stopped me and asked me if I'd seen their cat.

I frowned at Scatty Scudder. I knew her cat quite well because, being scatty, she was always running out of cat food and the cat – a skinny ginger one – would follow her to the shop and sit outside while she bought some.

"Not lately," I said, taking in her tea-cosy hat, her furry slippers and her moulting fur coat. "That's the ginga cat, right?"

"Ginga?" she said. "No, he's a lovely ginger colour. He wears a red collar with his name – Sooty – engraved on it."

Well, yes, I thought about it, but decided I couldn't face asking her why she'd called a ginga cat Sooty. It was just NFB.

"I thought I heard him meowing early this

morning but he never turned up for his breakfast, so I wondered if he'd got stuck inside someone's shed. I've asked all round but no one's seen him."

I promised that if I saw him I'd send him straight home, and carried on keepy-upping towards Mrs Huge-o's house, which was in a little lane running off the green. As I did so, I thought about what I was going to buy with the money I'd earn. A new England kit, for a start. And maybe a football video game. And some CDs and a few DVDs. "Morning, James," Mrs Huge-o said, looming up on me like a great big hot-air balloon as I went through her gates.

"Jake," I corrected her.

"You're rather late."

"Only seven minutes," I said. She was lucky I was there at all.

She didn't reply, but instead began to march up towards the house, pointing in all directions. "Now, this is what I want done: the vegetable patch must be dug over completely and all old roots removed, then the same procedure carried out with all the flower beds and, lastly, the borders."

I didn't have the least idea what she was talking about. "Where are all those, then?"

She pointed down the garden, sighing under her breath. "Rather obviously, the vegetable patch is where the vegetables are, the flower beds are where the flowers grow, and the borders, strangely enough, are on the borders of the garden. *Border* means *edge*."

"Whatever," I said, thinking it was no wonder her husband had gone away.

I took hold of the fork thing she'd given me and stuck it in the first bit of earth I saw. "I'll start here, then, shall I?"

She gave a scream. "No!" she said. "Not here. I don't want you to dig in this area *at all*!"

I looked at her curiously, wondering why she was going all red in the face just because I was about to dig up a few old twigs and bits of straw. "It's all garden, isn't it, and it's all got to be dug? What's the difference?"

"What's the difference?" she brayed. "This area right here is my precious patio garden, and I collect flowers from all over the world to plant in it."

"Oh, right," I said, thinking that it just looked like rubbish.

"So you must never dig in this area of ground near the house, James. Do you understand?"

"Jake," I said.

"Never, never, never!"

I looked at her consideringly. Jenna might be full-on psychic, but I get feelings of my own about things sometimes, and I was getting one right then. For old Huge-o to go *that* mad, there had to be a very important reason why she didn't want me to dig in her patio garden.

"OK," I said with fake chumminess, and then, to try and discover a bit more about her situation, added, "I'll try and make a good job of it. I can see how important the garden is to you and – your husband, is it?"

"Henry isn't here," she snapped.

"Oh."

"Don't let that concern you. He's working abroad with his job."

"Oh, that's nice. Which country?"

But I'd overstepped the mark there. "That's none of your business," she said, her flesh quivering indignantly. "Just get on with your digging."

I said nothing else to her, but moved down the path and stuck my fork in a different square of earth. She didn't roar at me this time, so I must have been in the right bit.

But as soon as ever I could, I thought to myself, *I was going to dig up that patio garden and discover whatever it was she didn't want me to find. . .*

CHAPTER THREE

After school on Wednesday Jenna and I were in my bedroom and kneeling up on the window seat, looking out over the green to see what was going on. The replica witch's house was coming along well and looked pretty authentic. Too authentic, maybe – not to say downright creepy – especially then, when it was getting dark and there was a faint mist coming up from the grass. There were some stalls being put up near it ready to sell food: potatoes in their jackets and hot dogs, and there was also going to be apple-bobbing and other games. A group of villagers were collecting junk ready for the bonfire and we could hear the sound of people chatting as they threw their bits of furniture on.

Jenna shook her head. "They all just think this pageant is a laugh," she said. "They haven't even wondered about the woman who was put to death, or realized they might be stirring up trouble for themselves." She got down from the window. "Oh, I almost forgot. I found out something about your Mr Huge-o today."

"What?" I asked eagerly.

"Well, for a start, he wasn't huge-o. Scatty Scudder told me that he was small and meek, and always at his wife's beck and call. She used to treat him like an errand boy, Scatty said."

"And where did he actually go? Or where does old Huge-o *say* he went?"

"Well, apparently, she put it about that he went abroad on a job with his firm and he never came back. Scatty said that they all thought it was very odd."

"*Very odd*. There you are!" I said. I'd been thinking about this quite a bit. "So, what if she's done away with him?"

"*Whhaat?*" Jenna said.

"I told you I thought she'd got something buried in her garden. Well, what if it's him: Mr Huge-o?"

Jenna shook her head. "I think you're going a bit NFB."

"You wait," I said. "I'm going to dig up her precious patio garden and find out." I bounced down from the window seat on to my bed. "When did you see Scatty, anyway?"

"Just now. She came to put a postcard in the shop window about her cat."

"He hasn't turned up, then?"

Jenna shook her head. "There are four postcards down there now. Mittens, Sooty, Tiddles and Fluffy: four different moggies missing."

"That's really strange," I said, and just as I said it, *at that very minute*, the big black cushion-cat walked into my bedroom.

I just gaped at it, but Jenna said hello, as if it was a nice cat, an ordinary cat, and sat down on the floor to stroke it.

I sniffed and pulled a face. "Does that have to come in here?"

"Sssshhh. It'll hear you and be offended." Jenna looked at the cat thoughtfully. "D'you think that maybe the other cats in the village are frightened of this new one?"

I shrugged. "Dunno."

"This is a big, powerful tom cat," Jenna said. "They're often a bit aggressive. Maybe he's made it clear he doesn't want any other cats around and they've all just scarpered."

"And maybe it's the real witch's cat, come back for a look-see before his mistress arrives. . ."

Jenna looked at me and raised her eyebrows. "Maybe he's that as well."

There was a shout from Mum, downstairs. "You two! Can you go and deliver a registered letter for me?"

I looked at the cat. "We'd better take that down with us and you can get it out of the door before Mum sees it."

As I spoke, the cat turned its cold grey eyes on me. It didn't like me, I could tell.

The letter we had to deliver was for a Mrs Wychwood, who'd only that week moved to the village. She lived in All Seasons Cottage between Miss Horseface Hall (hair like a mane, face like a mare) and Grouchy Green.

"Now, I want you both to be *very* polite to her," Mum said. "Tell her that the shop stocks everything she needs, and if she wants her foodstuffs brought to the house then we'd be delighted to deliver them."

"Seeing as I'm the delivery boy," I said, "I don't

know about *delighted*."

"Just you say it," said Mum.

I kicked along my football and parked it outside Mrs Wychwood's gate while Jenna rang the bell. It sounded strange. It didn't go *ding-dong* like normal bells, but gave an empty sort of clang.

"Like a death knell," Jenna said in a whisper.

"What's that?"

"The bell they ring at funerals," she said, then gave a little shriek and pointed to a bird sitting on the garden hedge. "And look at *that*!"

"A bird. So what?"

"It's a raven."

"Is it?" It looked like a great big sparrow to me. But then I reckon that all birds look like sparrows. They're just differently coloured and come in different sizes.

"Witches have those for their—" Jenna began saying, and just then the front door opened and a woman stood there. She was tall, had grey hair up in a bun and was wearing haggy black clothes. She had hard, glittering eyes and a pinched mouth.

Startled, Jenna thrust the envelope at her and I went into my smarmy "Hello our mum sent us

and we've got the shop and post office..."
routine, while she stared at us silently for a
moment, and then said, "Enter."

We entered. We were scared not to. The room
was quite bare, which was strange. I mean, the
rooms of the crinklies are usually stuffed with
bits: ornaments, books, framed photos, fluffy
animals, china frogs and so on, but her room
hardly had anything at all apart from a chair and
a small table.

"You live over the shop, you say?" she asked in
a flat voice.

Jenna nodded. "Our mum runs it."

I looked around. I didn't like it there; it was
cold and bare and I wanted to get out. I coughed
and nudged Jenna; she'd know what that meant.

"Have you a cold?" Mrs Wychwood asked me.

I shook my head.

"I think you have." She went into the kitchen
at the back, we heard some stirring and mixing,
then she came back in with some green liquid in
a glass. "You must take this."

"I haven't got a—" I began, but she glared at
me so forcefully, daring me to challenge her, that
I took the glass and swigged it back. It tasted
green and sharp – like the taste you get when you

chew the end of a bit of grass. Well, if I was poisoned I'd know who'd done it.

Jenna began to edge towards the door. "Don't forget – our shop opens at eight-thirty in the mornings."

"It closes at six and our half day is on Wednesdays. Goodbye!" I said, and we scrambled to get out of the front door as fast as we could.

"What an *odd* woman," Jenna said.

"Enormously odd," I agreed, giving my football a hefty kick. "And what were you going to say about that bird outside on her hedge?"

"Oh yes! Ratty told me this at the meeting last week: apparently it used to be thought that as well as a black cat, a witch would keep a raven – and sometimes a toad. They were her familiars and sometimes she would shape-shift between them."

"A raven and a cat. . ." I said, and then I gasped. "Course! I knew when she glowered at me that she reminded me of someone – that black cat! They've got the same cold, dead eyes."

"They have," Jenna agreed.

"I bet the cat's hers! I mean, she's the only new person in the village, so it must be!"

"And what about her name, Wychwood: *Witch Wood.*"

"Yeah! She can be Mrs Witch to us."

Jenna spoke hesitantly. "I wonder if maybe . . . maybe all this activity about the pageant and the burning has somehow rekindled Old Ma Morgan's power, and she's returned to the village, disguised as Mrs Wychwood." She stopped walking. "We really ought to go back and find out if she owns a black cat."

I groaned.

"You scared?"

"As if," I lied. "It's just . . . just. . ." But I couldn't really think of a good enough reason why we shouldn't, so I headed my football on to the wall of the dog pound and turned around to go back. "What'll we say?"

"Something will come to us," Jenna said. "We'll give her the opening hours of the shop."

"We've already told her those!"

"OK, we'll just ask her outright if she owns a cat. Nothing wrong with that – it's a perfectly natural question."

"Oh yeah, like: we think you're a witch – where's your black cat?"

"Sssh," Jenna said, because we were walking

up the path of All Seasons Cottage again by then. "Leave it to me."

When Mrs Witch opened the door, she didn't seem surprised to see us again. It was as if she'd been expecting us to return.

"We forgot to mention that Mum sells lots of varieties of cat food in the shop," Jenna said cheerily.

Mrs Witch didn't reply.

"Cat food," I said loudly, in case she was a bit deaf. "For your cat."

"What cat?"

"Well, we've seen a new black cat around. . ."

". . . and we thought it might be yours."

Mrs Witch looked at us coldly. "I do not keep a cat," she said, and closed the door on us.

We looked at each other as we went down the path. "Bet she does!" we said together. But quietly.

CHAPTER FOUR

The following afternoon after school, Jenna and I were in the shop when Mrs UFO (that is, Mrs Ulysses Farrington-Ocelot) came in carrying a large carrier bag full of packets of birdseed. She got them out and stood them along the counter one by one, while Mum, Jenna and I just stood and watched her.

"I think you've got the wrong idea," I began. "This is a shop."

"Jake. . ." Mum said warningly.

"That is, *we* sell *you* things," I explained.

Mrs UFO didn't flinch. "I'm returning this birdseed," she said, "because my Dave is no longer with us. At least, he *is* with us, but he's dead and not likely to be consuming any more Tweetie Birdseed, Caraway Variety Mix."

I could see Mum was a bit lost for words here. Well, weren't we all?

"I bought these packets from you last month," Mrs UFO went on. "It was a bulk buy and I thought it would be enough to feed Dave for the rest of his life. But now, tragedy has struck and I wish to return them."

"Dave is a bird?" Jenna asked.

"*Was* a bird," said Mrs UFO. "Dave was my canary."

"Ah," Mum said. She coughed delicately. "Won't you, perhaps, be having another canary?"

"Never!" said Mrs UFO. "After seeing poor Dave torn limb from limb – or perhaps that should be wing from wing – I'll *never* have a pet again."

"Who tore it wing from wing?" Jenna asked.

"A black cat! A great big, menacing black cat!" said Mrs UFO, and Jenna and I exchanged startled glances. "I put Dave's cage in the tree outside our door – he loved his fresh air, you know – and two minutes later I heard a commotion. When I went out there the cage was on the ground with its door open and all that was left of Dave were two yellow feathers. And then I saw a horrid black cat creeping off down the path."

"Oh dear. Yes, of course you can return the birdseed," Mum said. She nodded to me. "Put these packets back on the shelf, will you, Jake, and we'll try and resell them."

"I just don't want reminders of Dave in the house," said Mrs UFO. "You do understand, don't you?"

"Oh, certainly," Mum said soothingly.

"We've seen that black cat around the place quite a bit," Jenna said to Mrs UFO, "but no one seems to know who owns it."

"And it's frightened off half the village cats," I added, since two more postcards for missing cats, Binkie and Maisie, had joined the others on the noticeboard outside our shop.

"If I catch it," Mrs UFO said with more evil than you'd think possible in a dear little old lady, "I shall throw it in a sack and take it straight over to Mr Starr for stuffing."

The door banged behind her.

"Mrs UFO is clearly very NFB," said Jenna.

"What on earth does that mean?" Mum asked.

"It means she's barmy," I explained. "Or as we say – Normal for Bensbury."

"Well, that's not a very nice way to talk about our customers," Mum said. But she was grinning.

"Jake, about your role in the pageant," Mum said later when the shop had closed.

"What about it?" I asked suspiciously. "I haven't said I'll do anything yet."

She put down a plate of sausages and mash in front of me. "Well, Miss Ratcliffe popped in the shop this morning and suggested that you should be a firebrand."

"What's that?"

"I'm not certain," Mum said, "but something quite important, I'm sure. Something boyish," she said vaguely.

"I'm still going to be the village maiden, aren't I?" Jenna asked.

"Of course," Mum said. "I've nearly finished your costume. I've just got to find out what you'd be wearing on your head."

"And what does a firebrand wear?" I interrupted.

"I haven't been told," Mum said. "Miss

Ratcliffe said she would sort out the firebrand costumes herself."

"Costume*sssss*?" I said. "Aren't I the only firebrand on the block, then?"

"Obviously not!" Jenna said, all pleased with herself. "Not like me. I'm really important because I'm the *only* beautiful village maiden. . ."

I gave a snort of laughter. "A serious piece of miscasting, I think we're all agreed."

After we'd eaten and Mum had gone back into the post office to do some accounting work, Jenna dashed upstairs and brought down a small, old book bound in dark leather. "I've been waiting to show you this," she said. "I got it from Ratty today."

"What is it?"

"It's called *Witchfinding* – it's information about witches. Anything you ever wanted to know about them so that you can recognize them when you see them. And there's a special section about the ones living locally in the seventeenth century."

"Cool," I said.

She started leafing through it. "I think we ought to find out as much about witches as we can, so we can work out if Mrs Witch is a real one. There are certain things to look out for; certain details that witches have in common."

"The ones in *Buffy* always wear a five-pointed star so that they can recognize each other."

"This isn't TV," Jenna said witheringly, "this is real." She pointed to an illustration in the book. "It says here that witches can't cross running water. *That's* the sort of thing we want to know. We ought to find out as much as we can and then go to Mrs Witch's house and test her."

"Hmm." I thought for a moment. "If we do go, I reckon we should take the Reverend Whatsit with us. Then if we decide she *is* a witch, the rev can do that thing – you know, *exorcise* her. Cast the devils out."

Jenna nodded eagerly. "So let's get a piece of paper and go through the book listing everything we've got to look out for."

The list was as follows:

If Mrs Witch was a real witch she would:
1. Have a spellbook which she would keep near her at all times.
2. Not be able to cross running water.
3. Not have a reflection.

4. Have a clawmark under her left eye (possibly).
5. Have as her familiar a black cat, raven or toad into which she could shape-shift.
6. Be able to appear/disappear in a whirlpool of dust.
7. Have black candles about the place.
8. Often be seen at crossroads, or on ancient lanes where two paths cross.
9. Use the night of the full moon for special spells.
10. Have a crystal ball in which to see the future.
11. On ceremonial occasions, dance around in a circle with other witches.

We surveyed this list with satisfaction. "We'll let her settle in for a couple of days and then go over to her house and test her," I said.

But before we could do this, another Saturday came round and I had to go to Mrs Huge-o's and do more digging. She was just as painful as before, standing over me and saying I wasn't digging properly, that I needed to get air to the earth; break up the clods, aerate the soil, etc., etc. I didn't have the least idea what she was on about, so I just turned my back on her, stuck the fork in and hoped for the best.

I think she went inside for a bit, then she came out and said, "Now, James, I'm just going over to your mother's shop for some groceries."

"Jake."

"And I'd like you to have completed the vegetable garden by the time I get back."

I didn't speak, just kept digging.

She watched in silence for a moment, then she sighed heavily. "Oh dear, oh dear. I've told you before, James, you need to get a rhythm going: push the fork in, turn the soil over, pull the fork out. Get that? Push . . . turn . . . pull." She clapped her fat hands in time to what she was saying, "Push . . . turn . . . pull. Push . . . turn . . . pull. Come along now!"

Scowling heavily, I kept to my own pace, totally ignoring her clapping and her chanting. *Fat . . . old . . . bat*, I muttered in my head. *Fat . . . old . . . bat.*

At last she got fed up with my lack of response and went waddling off down the drive. As soon as I heard the metal gates clang shut behind her I left the fork where it was and dashed up to the patio garden with the spade. Then I started to dig very quickly all down one edge, carefully replacing any bits of old straw that looked like they might possibly be plants. It wasn't a very large plot and I reckoned it would only take me a couple of hours to dig it right over, so if I did a bit every time I came, and left some sort of marker to remind me of where I'd got to, then I'd soon be through it.

It was amazing how quickly I could do the digging thing when I wanted to, and the thought of catching Mrs Huge-o out in something underhand really spurred me on. I dug on steadily for ten minutes or so, carefully putting back any onion-looking things I unearthed, and was about to call it a day and return to where I was supposed to be when my spade suddenly made a *ching!* sound. It had struck something!

Cautiously, I bent down and looked carefully at the churned-up earth. It was something small and shiny. Some sort of coin, I thought at first, but then I got it out and rubbed it on my jeans and saw that it was the face and works of a man's watch. It was corroded away at top and bottom where the strap had joined, but after digging my fingers in the earth again and scrabbling about a bit, I found the gold-coloured expanding wristband which had once been attached to it. It was an old-fashioned-looking watch, the sort you had to wind up ... probably the sort that Mr Huge-o would have worn.

But who went abroad without taking their watch, and why was it buried here?

I heard the clang of the gate which signalled Mrs Huge-o's return and shoved the watch in my jeans pocket. Quick as a Rooney, I darted down to the vegetable garden and, positioning myself a short distance from where I'd been standing before, began digging the fork in and turning the earth over.

"Push ... turn ... pull," I murmured to myself. "Push ... turn ... pull. Oh!" That last bit was me pretending to be surprised as her huge figure loomed up on me.

"Done all that, have you?" she asked, inspecting the ground and frowning.

"Yeah," I said. "Once you get a rhythm going, it's quite easy."

"Quite," she said. "Carry on, James!"

I said nothing. She was doing it deliberately, I was sure of it. Never mind – I patted my pocket – I'd already found poor old Mr Huge-o's watch. And maybe, if I kept digging, I'd find him. . .

CHAPTER FIVE

"I don't know," Jenna said, opening her eyes. She was holding the watch I'd found – the watch I was sure was Mr Huge-o's – in her hand. "I'm not sure if it's his or not."

"Try again," I urged her. I hadn't managed to get any vibes from it at all and she was usually much better at the psychic stuff than I was.

She shut her eyes again and closed her fingers over the watch. "Mr Hugo – is this yours?" she said, and then sat for so long without moving that I thought she'd gone to sleep.

"Well?" I asked in the end. "What's happening? You must be getting something."

"Don't be so impatient! It isn't like tuning in a radio," she said. "And anyway, I'm not."

"Not getting *anything*?"

"No. I already told you I wasn't. You can't *make* yourself feel stuff, it just comes."

I groaned. *Fat lot of good you are*, I wanted to say. *Call yourself psychic*? But I didn't, of course, because I didn't want my hair pulled out by its roots.

The week following was half-term, with the pageant taking place on the final Saturday of the month. Pumpkins had been carved into faces and put into all the cottage windows overlooking the green – we had three in the shop window – and details of the pageant had been put on the tourist websites. We'd heard there were loads of people coming (fairly alarming thought, this, considering I was being a firebrand and hadn't got the faintest idea what they did). In the meantime, the bonfire was getting bigger, last-minute touches were being made to the witch's hovel, and people who had a speaking part in the pageant were learning their lines. We had half the village coming into the shop muttering to themselves, *not* because they were completely mad (although most of them were, obviously), but because they were practising what they had to say on the night. A firebrand, apparently, didn't have any lines to learn, but Jenna had already learned hers and kept spouting them at every opportunity.

On Monday I was having a bit of a kickabout on the green, trying to keep well away from the witch's hovel and, in fact, not even looking at it because it looked much too real. If I let myself think about it I could still see that etching, with the shady figure of the witch standing outside and shaking her fist. . .

My ball went off on a tangent, though, and I had to get a bit closer to the hovel than I wanted to retrieve it. I heard a voice calling, "Jake! Oh, Jake!" and I was just about to freak out, abandon the kickabout and run for home when the door of the hovel opened and Ratty came out.

"Oh sorry, did I startle you?" she asked.

I shook my head, whistling carelessly.

"Only you've gone awfully pale."

"Nah," I said. "I'm just out of breath. Been doing some heavy football training."

She looked at me closely. "You didn't think it was the witch calling to you, did you?" she asked, and then she laughed heartily and I laughed too. Or tried to.

"Well, dear," she said when she stopped, "I was just checking up on the bits and pieces inside and I realized that we didn't have a witch's cat. I saw you and thought you could pop over to Mr Starr's house and get a stuffed one."

"Right!" I said. I liked going to Stuffer Starr's seriously weird house. "I'll go now, shall I?"

She nodded. "Tell him that we'll keep it safe and he can have it back after the pageant."

Stuffer lived in a cottage in Meadow View, next door to Mr Tragic the magician, and in order to get past *his* house without being forced to go in and watch him cut a lady in half or to have a tap stuck on my head, I crept by on all fours below the level of his wall.

Stuffer was ages answering his front door and I thought he was probably in what he called his surgery, cutting up animals and doing the stuffing of them. I didn't want to think too much about that, though, *or* look at his hands when he eventually appeared and ushered me inside.

"So what is it, lad?" he asked when we were in the sitting room.

"Ratty ... er ... Miss Ratcliffe wants to borrow a cat for the pageant," I said, staring around at all the animals. It was *mad* in there:

46

like some weird sort of jungle where birds and bears sat alongside stoats and badgers, and every animal seemed to be weirdly suspended in time.

"How about a nice big ginger tom?" he said, pointing to the stuffed cat curled up on a cushion by the fireplace.

I shook my head. "It's for the witch's cat," I said, and I went a little closer to the ginga cat just to make sure it wasn't Scatty's.

"You'll be wanting a black cat, then."

I nodded. "A wicked-looking one if you've got one."

"I've seen a *very* wicked-looking one skulking around the place lately – a great bruiser of a black cat. Stuff up a treat, that would!"

"We've seen that one, too," I said, "but no one seems to own it." I looked around the room. "And a lot of the ordinary village cats have disappeared."

"You needn't look in here," he said. "I only do road kill and special requests. I don't go stealing moggies from doorsteps."

"No. Course not," I said. I looked into the aviary, where a great variety of differently coloured and differently sized sparrows were suspended from wires pretending to fly, or sitting on twigs not moving as much as a feather. "Maybe a raven would do instead. Have you got one of those? Or a toad?"

"I didn't say I hadn't *got* a black cat," said Stuffer. "It's just that Silky is a particular favourite and I don't like her going out of the house."

"She's only going to sit in the doorway of the witch's house," I said. "Miss Ratcliffe will make sure she's all right."

He bent down and opened a tall, glass-fronted cupboard. "Well, I suppose you can have her, then," he said, handing me a wooden plinth on which sat a stuffed and sleek black cat. "You tell Miss Ratcliffe to keep an eye on her, though."

"She looks too nice to be a witch's cat," I said, looking admiringly at Silky.

"She *is* too nice. She was a very well-to-do cat. An aristocat – ha ha!"

I laughed dutifully. "How did you get her?"

He tapped his nose. "That's for me to know and you to wonder. Now, off you go and let me get on with my work."

* * *

"Hmm," Ratty said when I produced Silky from under my arm. "Has it got to stay on that piece of wood?"

"I think so," I said. "He didn't really want to let you have her at all. He said she's his particular favourite."

"He says that about all of them. Put it over there by the witch's door then, will you, Jake – next to the broom. And put some grass around the bottom to hide the base. Make it look natural, as if it's sitting there waiting for the witch to come home."

I shivered when she said that, and when I got over to the witch's house, I couldn't bring myself to look in the windows just in case she was there – the old woman Jenna and I had seen in the drawing in her raggedy black dress and cloak, shaking her fist at us.

I bent down and arranged some grass around the cat, pulling in longer strands to hide the pale wood of her stand. *Look in the window*, I urged myself. *What are you scared of? A witch is just a daft old woman with a tall hat and a broom.*

"Ow!" I gave a sudden yell as I thought that last bit, because while I'd been pulling up grass I'd somehow pulled up a nettle, too, and it had stung me right across my fingers and palm. "Ow-ow!"

"They can hurt you, can't they?" a voice said. I looked round, ready to say something sarcastic, but the words died on my lips when I saw Mrs Witch standing there looking at me with those stone-grey eyes of hers.

"You can rub a dock leaf on to it," she said. "Or turn round three times under an elm tree to ease the pain."

"That's OK," I said, hastily getting to my feet. "It's only a sting."

"Several stings, I think," she said. "If you come to my cottage I'll give you a herbal salve."

"Nah, that's OK," I said hastily. "Gotta be going, anyway."

I'd already started backing off when Ratty came up. "I don't think I've had the pleasure," she said, looking at Mrs Witch.

"Ida Wychwood," said Mrs Witch. "Recently moved into All Seasons Cottage."

"Ah, yes," said Ratty, twitching her pointy nose. "And how fortunate that you've come just in time for our pageant. Perhaps you'd like to take a small part in it?"

"Indeed I would not," said Mrs Witch, and just

turned on her heel and went off across the green without another word.

Ratty tutted indignantly. "Well! How very rude!"

"Yeah," I nodded. "Me and Jenna think she's a bit . . . weird."

"Has she come to live in Bensbury alone? Because if she carries on in *that* vein she's going to find herself with no one to speak to."

"She might have a cat with her – we're not sure."

"Not *another* cat in the village!" said Ratty, pulling a face.

I grinned to myself. So the ratty one didn't like cats. Pretty obvious one, that. "It's just that we thought that the big new mog which has frightened off all the village cats might be hers, because they both seemed to arrive here at the same time. When we asked her, though, she said it wasn't."

"She probably knows it's a bully and doesn't want to admit she owns it."

"Yeah, that's what we reckoned." I hesitated, and then thought I might as well get it over with. "About me being a firebrand," I asked, "what actually *is* one and what will I have to do?"

"Come over to my house later in the week and

I'll tell you all about it. And your costume should be ready by then, too."

"Is it an ... er ... good sort of part?" I asked tentatively. "Only I'm better known as a footballer than an actor."

"Oh, you'll just love being a firebrand!" she said. Which didn't reassure me one bit.

At some unearthly hour in the middle of that night, Jenna came running into my bedroom and bounced my mattress up and down until I woke up.

"Jake! The bonfire!" I dimly heard her say.

"Wha' about it?"

"It's going up!" she said excitedly.

"Up? In the air?" I asked sleepily, visualizing a big pile of sticks floating away.

"No! It's alight! Look – it's amazing!" She shook me a bit more, and then she put her icy cold hand down my back and refused to take it away until I got out of bed.

In the end I managed to haul myself out, prop myself against the window and look over the green, and immediately saw the amazing, startling sight of the bonfire engulfed in red, gold, orange and silver flames. "Oh, wow!" I breathed.

"I *told* you! I heard a crackling noise and I couldn't work out what was going on. Then I saw flames reflected on my ceiling, looked out of the window and there it was!"

"There it *wasn't*," I corrected her, as the bonfire was burning with such bright and fierce flames that it looked as if it might disappear within moments.

"D'you think we ought to tell anyone?"

I shook my head. "It's not close enough to anything to catch it alight, and anyway, the rate it's going, it'll all be over before anyone can do anything."

"There'll be no bonfire for Guy Fawkes' Night, then."

I shrugged. "They've got over a week to go yet. They'll be able to collect more stuff."

We stood at the window watching for several more minutes and then Jenna said, "I know this is a silly question, but d'you think this bonfire we're looking at is the *same* bonfire?"

"What're you on about?"

"Is it exactly where it was before?"

"What d'you mean?"

"What I mean," she said, "is that *this* one seems closer to us. I thought the bonfire was in the middle of the green, but this looks like it's nearer."

"You're crazy. Anyway, you can't tell how far away anything is . . . it's all pitch-black out there apart from the fire."

"This is true."

We stood there watching for another five minutes or so until the flames had eaten through the piled-up junk and there was barely anything left.

"I wonder how it started?" Jenna asked.

I yawned and was just about to say that I hadn't the faintest when outside the big black cat strode into view. For a moment its bulky shape was silhouetted on the glowing embers of the bonfire, where it threw a long, wavering shadow, then it disappeared into the darkness again.

"How did it start?" I said. "There's your answer. Bet that cat and its owner had something to do with this. . ."

CHAPTER SIX

The following morning I was just about awake when I heard a scream from Jenna's room. I ran in, thinking that at the very least she was being attacked by vampires, but she was only standing on her bed staring out of the window. "It's still there!" she cried.

"What is?"

"The bonfire! Look!"

I jumped up on to her bed to see what she was on about, then just gawped at the sight in front of us. The bonfire *was* still there, piled high with wood and pallets and cardboard boxes and everything else that people had been throwing on it for the last couple of weeks. It was just as high as it had been before – I even recognized an empty wooden crate I'd chucked on the previous evening.

"Blimey," I said. "Not as much as a scorch mark."

"That's crazy!"

I breathed deeply. "It must have been one of your weird visions, somehow transferred to me. . ."

She shivered. "Remember that black cat walking in front of it?"

"Course I do."

We were silent for a while, and then Jenna said, "I wonder if Mrs Witch is behind all this?"

I nodded. "I think you were right saying what you did when we first met her: that she might be a reincarnation of Old Ma Morgan, returned to the village for her anniversary."

Jenna nodded, then screwed up her face, puzzled. "It's just weird that I'm not getting any real vibes about her."

"Maybe she's *so* powerful that she can stop vibes and in that way prevent people from discovering who she really is," I suggested. Then I thought for a moment and added, "I think we ought to try and sort her out. We could do what we said – contact the rev and get him to come round to her house with us."

Jenna nodded. "OK. We'll get over there as soon as we can."

Because loads of people were expected to come to the village for the pageant, Mum intended to keep the shop open later that Saturday. She'd ordered stacks of extra food to sell: crisps, snacks, fifty varieties of choc bar, etc., so most of that morning we were busy unpacking the crates and boxes which had arrived from the wholesalers.

When Ratty came in the shop, Jenna asked her if she'd heard anything strange in the night.

"Not a thing," she said. "Why?"

"Because . . . because we thought we heard a fire crackling."

"And it sounded a bit like the bonfire had ignited on its own," I added.

She twitched her nose a little. "Well, what overactive imaginations you've both got!"

Jenna thought for a moment, then said, "Miss Ratcliffe, is this bonfire in the same place as the original one?"

Ratty frowned slightly. "Well, it's funny you should ask that."

Mum's tut of disapproval carried across the

shop. "Twins! Do stop bothering Miss Ratcliffe with all your questions. I'm sure she's much too busy with the pageant right now to listen to you."

"Not at all," Ratty said. She put her shopping in her wheely-bag and added, "If you come outside with me I'll show you something."

She led us a short way across the green and pointed to a ring of darkened grass; a near-perfect circle which could only be seen if you stared at the ground hard. "Legend has it that *this* is the exact spot where the original bonfire was, four hundred years ago. Where Old Ma Morgan died."

"Wow," Jenna and I said together.

"I thought, though, that it would be rather unseemly to have our pageant jollities where someone actually died, so I decided our bonfire should be further towards the middle of the green."

Jenna looked at me.

"I mean, it's probably just coincidence that the grass is still discoloured and tainted on this spot, but . . . well, you never know, do you?" And off she went, trailing her trolley behind her.

We stared at the circle. "I told you!" Jenna

said. "I *thought* the one we saw last night was closer!"

"Yeah, you were right." I nodded. "The bonfire we saw in flames – the apparition – was, from our window, slap-bang in front of the real one and so obscured it from view. And it was too dark to see anything else anyway."

"So d'you think what we saw in the middle of the night was a re-enactment of the *real* witch-burning. . . ?"

"Could be," I said, and I felt a cold shiver all down my back.

Late that afternoon we went over to the village church to find the reverend. This rev wasn't at all the way you'd think a rev would be. Firstly he was a laugh, secondly he was about fifty years younger than anyone else in the village, thirdly and best of all he knew his football, so was the only person in the village I could talk to about The Game.

He and I had a short discussion on the new understanding of the Offside Rule while Jenna screamed and put her hands over her ears, and then we told him what we thought about the pageant, and the mysterious black cat, and Mrs

Wychwood being some sort of reincarnation of Old Ma Morgan. His face grew more and more incredulous with each thing we said, and when we'd finished he burst out laughing.

"Oh, come on!" he said.

"But her moving in right *now*. . ."

"And all the cats disappearing. . ."

"And her making potions and having spells against nettle stings. . ."

"And discovering a raven outside her house. . ."

"And seeing that bonfire alight!"

As we paused for breath he shook his head. "It's hardly enough for the ref to show her a red card."

"But please, couldn't you just come across to her house with us?" Jenna asked.

I bounced my football hard on the church wall. "We could have a bit of a kickabout on the way. . ."

"Just see what you think," Jenna wheedled. "And if you *do* think she's a witch, then perhaps you could exorcise her."

The rev laughed again. "Jenna, love, it's not the Middle Ages."

"They do it on *Buffy*," I pointed out.

"It need only be a very *small* exorcism," Jenna pleaded. "For the good of the village."

"She needn't even know you're doing it."

"OK," he said, grinning all over his face, "I'll come over there with you. But not to find out if she's a witch – to welcome her to the village."

He went inside to get himself ready. "If she asks us in, look for her spell book," Jenna said. "And a crystal ball or a talisman of some sort."

I nodded. "And see if there are any mirrors around for her *not* to be reflected in. And if she's wearing a five-pointed star."

"If she's a witch," Jenna said, "she's hardly going to be advertising the fact."

"They do on *Buffy*," I muttered.

Twenty minutes or so later we were standing outside All Seasons Cottage. So that she – Mrs Witch – wouldn't wonder why Jenna and I had turned up with him, the rev had given us things to carry: Jenna had a box containing six eggs from his chickens and I had a collecting box for the restoration of the church spire, plus a list of church activities for the coming weeks.

"Mrs Wychwood?" the rev said when she opened the door.

Mrs Witch nodded. She was, I thought, looking particularly witch-like that afternoon, with her long grey hair hanging all anyhow down her back. I looked for warts on her nose and chin but, disappointingly, couldn't see any.

"I've just called with a couple of our young residents to welcome you to the village and wish you a long and comfortable stay here," said the rev, and I rattled the collecting box.

She didn't say anything for a moment and I longed for the rev to hold up a cross in front of her and watch her fall to the ground and shrivel into dust.

"Thank you for that," she said quite primly, and went to close the door.

"I hope we may see you in church soon," the rev said quickly. "But if not, perhaps you'll be interested in joining the Women's Institute, or the Foreign Aid meetings, or one of our stamp-collecting sessions."

For each thing he mentioned she shook her head. Well, I thought, you couldn't blame the woman for that. He wasn't exactly offering tickets for Arsenal v. Man U, was he?

"We also hold poetry readings and certain other. . ."

All the while he was speaking I was looking behind Mrs Witch, my eyes zipping across the room for evidence. I couldn't see any spellbooks, though, or black mirrors, crystal balls or talismans. I certainly couldn't see any chalked circles that witches might dance around with their broomsticks. No, she was being very careful indeed.

I gasped. What she *hadn't* been careful about, though, was the cat. The big black cushion-cat, perched on the back of the easy chair in the room and looking very much at home. "Yay!" I said before I could stop myself.

Everyone looked at me.

"It's the cat! The . . . er . . . lovely black cat," I said, pointing at it. I looked at her enquiringly. "I didn't think you had a cat, Mrs Wychwood."

"I have not. There is no cat," she said flatly, and with her foot she pushed open the front door a little more and turned round to indicate the room.

She was right; there was no cat to be seen. During that moment, that tiny moment when my view of the room had been obliterated, it had disappeared.

That made me look more than a bit stupid. I

mean, as I said to Jenna as we walked home, I could hardly barge in and start demanding to look under beds and things, could I?

She shook her head. "And anyway, the rev didn't believe us, did he?"

"Nope." The rev had said that Mrs Wychwood was a funny old woman, a funny, ill-mannered, *weird* old woman, but he didn't think she was a witch. He might have said more about it, but as we were coming away from her house, Mrs UFO had pounced on us.

"I'm very pleased I've seen you," she said to the rev. "I wondered if you'd officiate at a funeral and find a small place in your graveyard for my Dave."

The rev looked startled. "Of course, Mrs Farrington-Ocelot," he said. "But, do forgive me, I hadn't realized any of your household were ill. Was it an accident?"

"Oh, it was no accident!" she said. "A great brute saw my Dave, stalked him and bit him."

The rev was very taken aback. "Bit him? Killed him? A *murder*?"

She nodded. "And now he's gone to that great aviary in the sky."

The rev went pale.

"Dave was her canary," Jenna put in. "And he was killed by the cat. The *witch's* cat," she added in an undertone.

"Ah. I ... er ... see," said the rev, looking relieved. "You had me there for a moment." He seemed to rally himself. "But I'm afraid even birds with human names can't be buried in churchyards." He looked at us and added in an undertone, "And there are no such things as witches."

We didn't say anything. We knew better.

CHAPTER SEVEN

"Yes, the bread's just been delivered at the shop,"
I said to Mrs Huge-o on Wednesday morning.
"Fresh rolls, buns, cakes, pies." I looked up and
down at the great size of her. "*Who ate all the*
pies. . .? Who ate all the pies. . .?" I sung under
my breath.

"What's that?" she asked sharply.

"Just a football song," I said. "No, you'd best
get over to the shop smartish if you want the
freshly baked stuff, because it gets sold really
quickly, especially on half-day closing."

Go, I thought to myself. *Go so I can have*
another dig in the patio garden and find
something else of your husband's. Or your
husband himself. . .

She went, eventually, after telling me that what I'd done the previous time hadn't been done quite well enough and she wanted me to re-dig in certain places and aerate the soil and all that stuff I didn't know anything about. I said I'd do it while she was out, and eventually she went off. She was wearing a dark grey woolly coat and, as she lumbered across the green, looked like a dark raincloud passing over the horizon.

As soon as she was gone I jumped out of the trench I was digging, ran quite smartish up to the patio garden and started forking it over as before, in a line from the top to the bottom. I didn't really expect to find anything else, not so quickly, but almost as soon as I got level with the spot where I'd found the watch, my fork gave another *ching!*

I hesitated for a couple of minutes before going on because, much as I wanted to get Mrs Huge-o into trouble, I didn't fancy finding a skeleton. We'd already come across one in Bensbury and it hadn't been nice.

I hesitated a bit longer, talking myself up, then stuck a prong of the fork in the ground and cautiously scraped at the earth where I'd heard the *ching*. In just two scrapes I'd uncovered it: an oblong, silvery thing, about half as big as a paperback book, engrained with dirt. I shoved it quickly into the pocket of my jeans, my heart hammering, and raked over the earth where I'd been digging.

What had I found? I didn't know. Something of Mr Huge-o's, I was sure, and I'd look at it as soon as I got home.

I went back to the trench where Mrs Huge-o had left me digging. When she returned from the shop about twenty minutes later, she was as appreciative as ever about what I'd done.

"Oh dear, oh dear," she said (after putting on different glasses, all the better to inspect my work). "You don't take a pride in what you do, do you, James? I fear that you'll never make a gardener."

"Well, that's lucky," I said, "because I intend to be a Premiership footballer."

She looked at her watch. "I'm going out shortly and I want to lock my gates, so I'm afraid you'll have to finish now."

"That's all right with me!" I said, throwing down my tools.

"So let's see; you've only been here twenty-five minutes – you were late, of course – so I can hardly pay you for an hour's work." She sniffed. "Most of it was for redoing what you should have done properly last time, so I think we'll just call it quits, shall we?"

"No, I don't think we will!" I began, but she'd already begun lumbering off towards the house. "Excuse me!" I yelled after her, but she merely waved her fat arm at me.

Furious, I jumped out of the trench. And then I stopped. I could have gone after her and had a real go, but if I did, I knew I'd get into trouble with Mum. Besides, I was keen to get home and investigate the silver object.

Going back towards the shop, I bumped into Grouchy Green, muttering and moaning to himself. "Bloody stupid idea – this pageant," he said on seeing me. "Waste of time and energy. Better to spend some time clearing up dog's muck."

I was about to murmur something in reply, when it suddenly struck me to find out what he thought about Mr and Mrs Huge-o. "Excuse me for asking," I said in my best speaking-to-crinklies voice, "but did you know Mr Hugo?"

"What you want to know for?" he growled.

"Only because I'm . . . er . . . doing some work

for Mrs Hugo and I wondered what he . . . what she. . ." I said, floundering.

"You're wondering how that old battleaxe could ever get a man in the first place, I daresay."

I grinned. "Yup!"

"That's what we all wondered. She used to treat her husband – old Henry – like her dog! He did everything for her bar run across to the shop and come back with a newspaper in his mouth."

"Oh," I said.

"Once upon a time he would come over to the Unicorn for a pint, but she put a stop to that. And I'll tell you something else, too. . ."

I nodded encouragingly.

"She put it about that he stayed abroad with his job, but I don't believe he did." He winked at me. "Know what I mean?"

I winked back, nodding. I didn't have the slightest idea.

Did he mean that he, too, thought she'd done away with him? Was I really going to find Mr Huge-o buried in the patio garden?

"It's a cigarette case," said Mum when I brought the object out of my pocket later. "People don't have them much nowadays." She leant over the kitchen table to look at it. "It's a bit tarnished, but it could be silver."

"Let's have a look," Jenna said, and she took the case, felt around the edge of it and located a catch which she pressed. The case sprung open, revealing a gold-coloured interior and a few threads of tobacco.

"Here, clean it up a bit," Mum said, handing me a piece of kitchen roll.

I did so, and discovered an ornate, swirly design engraved on the top: a circle with the letters *HH* inside.

"Henry Hugo!" Jenna said, leaning closer to see.

"Mum, would a man move away without taking his watch and cigarette case?" I asked.

She thought for a moment. "I shouldn't think so," she said. "But perhaps he left in a hurry. Of course, that case really belongs to Mrs Hugo now. You'll have to take it back, Jake. Say you found it where you were digging."

I didn't say anything; I had no intention of letting old Huge-o know I'd been digging where I shouldn't have been.

As Mum swanned off to do something at the other end of the kitchen, Jenna and I exchanged glances. "I reckon she must have killed him," I said in a low voice.

"I dunno," Jenna said. She looked thoughtful. "I'm not actually getting any psychic messages or bad feelings about it. . ."

"Well, maybe you're not functioning properly in the psychic messages department."

"What are you two whispering about?" Mum asked. Talk about having the hearing of Superman.

"Nothing!" we both said together.

"Don't forget you've got to go to Miss Ratcliffe's tonight, Jake."

I looked at Mum darkly. "Being a firebrand had *better* be all right. . . "

"So what actually have I got to do?" I asked Ratty.

"And what has he got to wear?" added Jenna, who'd come to her house to see the fun.

"Well, it's quite simple," Ratty said. "At the end of the play, the beautiful maiden ties up the witch and pretends to light the bonfire, but as we aren't actually lighting it until Guy Fawkes' Night, it will be up to you, Jake, to simulate flames. And as we haven't been able to find anyone else to be a firebrand with you, you're the only one."

"Hmm," I said. "And what does a firebrand do, exactly?"

A moment later I was wishing I hadn't asked, because Ratty got up from her chair, stretched up her arms and did the most embarrassing movements you've ever seen, worse than your old aunty dancing at a disco. *Much* worse. She shook her arms, swayed her body, contorted her face and wriggled her legs in the most grisly, painful display you've ever seen. "See! I'm a flame! I'm a flickering flame! I'm a shivering, flimmering, quivering flame!" she cried.

Jenna and I were absolutely speechless, then Jenna dissolved into giggles and I had to nudge her hard to shut up.

Still shivering and quivering, Ratty wriggled over to the far side of her sitting room calling, "I'm a gleaming, glistening flame!" as she went. She took something from the back of a chair and came wriggling back towards me, arms flailing. "Here's your outfit," she said, holding it in front of me.

"I don't *think* so," I said, staring at the outfit in horror. It was very, *very* orange; a sort of nightie affair with raggedy, flame-shaped bits sewn all over and glittery sequin things around the hem. "I'm not wearing that!" I said. "And I'm not dancing like that, either. Not in your wildest dreams."

"Mum won't like it," Jenna said on our way home. "If you refuse to be in it she'll go off on one."

"Never mind that," I said, "what about my street cred? I'm not dressing up in an orange nightie for *anyone*."

As we walked across the green, the witch's house loomed closer in the darkness. We were about to make a wide journey around it when Jenna suddenly stopped walking. "Is it just my imagination," she asked, staring towards it, "or can you hear a funny noise coming from there?"

I stopped too. "I can't hear anything," I said.

"A sort of. . ." she put her head on one side, ". . . ripping or tearing noise. Shall we go and see if there's anything going on?"

"Leave off!" I said. "I've had enough of that witch and her pageant for one night."

"No, I think we ought to. We might discover Mrs Witch inside there doing spells."

I sighed, groaned a bit, but in the end went with her.

We crept up to the window and tried to look in, but inside the hut it was as black as the inside of a wolf's mouth.

"So what was that noise you heard?"

Jenna shrugged, mystified. We walked around towards the wooden door and it was then that we saw Silky, Stuffer's best cat, with her head ripped off and all the straw pulled out of her.

"*That* was the noise," Jenna said as we stared down at the decimated cat on the ground. "Silky being pulled to bits."

"Oh, hell," I said, "we'd better go back and tell Ratty."

"And *she* can be the one to tell Stuffer."

CHAPTER EIGHT

Mum, me and Jenna were all in the shop the following morning when Grouchy Green came in, moaning his head off the minute he opened the door.

"Blasted things!" he said. "*Flies!* Whoever heard of flies in October?"

"What's that, Mr Green?" Mum asked.

"There's a swarm of flies on the green," he said. "A clump as big as a cloud! I had to put my coat over my head and run through them, or the little blighters would have settled on me."

Jenna and I exchanged startled glances and I knew we were both thinking the same thing: hadn't someone in Old Ma Morgan's time said they'd been cursed by a swarm of flies?

Grouchy went over to the post office counter. "Flies, now!" I said to Jenna in a low voice. "D'you think that's just a coincidence?"

"Dunno," Jenna shrugged. "It's Grouchy, after all. If he gets two spots of rain on him, he'll complain he's been in a monsoon."

"Let's see if anyone else mentions them."

Ten minutes later Ratty came in, coughing, shaking her head and picking things off her fluffy coat. "I've got those nasty little beasts all over me!" she said.

We looked at her enquiringly.

"Flies! A horrid great swarm of them hanging around the green."

"Don't you think that's a bit strange?" I asked Ratty.

"Certainly I do! Flies at the end of October – *very* strange."

"Not just that," I said. "You told us about someone in the olden days being cursed with a swarm of flies, and now it's happened again."

"D'you think it might be something to do with the pageant?" Jenna asked.

Ratty looked at us as if we were barking. "Lord above, no!" she said. "It's just a coincidence. Nothing more, nothing less." She rummaged in her bag. "Now, I've bought over a small poster which I'd like you to put in your window."

"Certainly," Mum said. "Is it something to do with the pageant?"

"It's something to do with the *cat*," Ratty said. "The big black tom prowling about the village. I think it was him who attacked Mr Starr's Silky. He's frightfully cross about it."

The notice read:

WANTED – DEAD OR ALIVE
Large black tom cat with bitten ears.
Believed to have frightened off several
of our village cats, killed a canary and
to have savaged "Silky" belonging
to Mr Starr. Anyone seeing the
above-mentioned animal is asked to
trap it in their home and call the vet
immediately to have it taken away.

"Have it taken away by the vet – that's a bit drastic," Jenna mumured.

"Well, I'm afraid it's got to be," Ratty said. "We can't have our village being terrorized by a feline."

The poster was stuck in the shop window next

to the Missing Cat notices and while Ratty tried to remember what else she'd come to the shop for, I took the opportunity to repeat what I'd said the night before: that I didn't intend – no *way* did I intend – to be a firebrand in a frilly flame outfit. There was a bit of a relegation tussle between us, but eventually she agreed that a firebrand might possibly wear an orange T-shirt instead (which I didn't mind, being Holland's football team colour). I also said to her that I wasn't going to be *quivery*, *flimmery* or anything of that nature, but might be willing to do a sort of Native American dance, like they did around their camp fires. I could have just ducked out on the whole pageant, of course, but it wasn't worth the aggro I'd have got from Mum.

And in the meantime I had something else on my mind.

"What happens to someone's mail when they die?" I said to Mum while we were having lunch. "Where do their letters go?"

"Well, whatever sort of a question's that?"

"I was just wondering. . ."

Wondering about Mr Huge-o, actually, and trying to find out how Mrs Huge-o had disposed of him. Gone abroad with his job, had he? I didn't believe that for a minute.

"Well," Mum said, "I think their letters would probably go to where they used to live and then their next of kin would deal with them."

"And what if they just moved away from a place?"

Mum looked at me, pleased. "It's nice that you're taking an interest in the work of the post office," she said, making Jenna smirk at me behind her peanut butter sandwich. "Well, if people move house, they usually fill in a special form at their local post office and then all their mail gets forwarded to the new address. They have to pay for that service, of course."

"So if someone moved from here – from Bensbury – then we'd have their new address?"

Mum nodded.

"Even if it was abroad?"

"Of course. Although it would be strictly confidential," she said. "A customer's personal details could never be disclosed to anyone else."

"Oh," I said. I gave Jenna a look. It was her turn to ask something, just in case Mum was getting suspicious.

"Strictly confidential? What, you have to

keep all those sorts of details in the safe or something?" she asked Mum.

Mum was, as usual, trying to do six things at the same time, so didn't seem to notice that she was being grilled. "What? Oh no, they'd just be in the general records."

Jenna kicked me under the table, nodding to the filing cabinet in the corner, and I nodded back. Later, Jenna could keep Mum occupied while I had a quick riffle through. . .

"So it doesn't look as if he went abroad with his firm," Jenna said. "At least we know that now."

I nodded thoughtfully. Much to our surprise, there *had* been a forwarding address for Mr Huge-o; any letters received in Bensbury were being redirected to a Jasmine Cottage in Grimbridge, the next village.

And we were on the bus heading there right then.

"So he may not be dead after all."

"Bet he is!" I said, rather reluctant to give up the idea that Mrs Huge-o had done away with him and buried him. "She's just having his letters sent on there so no one gets suspicious. Maybe she owns a house in both villages."

"Well, we'll soon find out," said Jenna.

Grimbridge, we realized when we got there, was pretty much like Bensbury, with village green, public house, twee cottages, and so on, except – big deal – it had two shops instead of our one. We stopped a woman in the street to ask where Jasmine Cottage was, and she told us to go up a small road which led up a hill, and Jasmine Cottage was the end one of three.

"This isn't half the size of Mrs Huge-o's house," I said as we stood outside looking at it.

"Hers is more like a mansion!"

The garden, too, was just an ordinary one with bushes and grass and stuff. Not like Mrs Huge-o's great park of a place. We walked down the path and knocked at the front door.

No one came and I knocked again, then for a third time, much louder. We waited a while, then just as I was thinking of going to the house next door and asking who lived in Jasmine Cottage, Jenna tilted her head as if she was listening to something. "Wait! I can hear voices. . ."

"Spirit voices?" I asked hopefully.

"No, garden voices," she said. "Someone's around the back."

We banged on the side gate and as no one

answered, opened it and went down the passageway. I could hear the voices, too, now: a man and a woman's, floating out to us through the greenery.

I coughed a sort of *excuse-me-for-interrupting* cough and stuck my head around the end of the cottage. Then I just stood and gaped. And so did Jenna.

What we saw was a wooden hot tub on a boarded-over area just outside the house. Steam was rising from the tub in clouds, and sitting inside it were an elderly man wearing a funny puffed-up shower cap, and a woman who looked quite a bit younger, wearing a swimming hat decorated with pink plastic flowers. They hadn't heard my cough because they were laughing so much.

"Excuse me!" Jenna called.

I coughed again. "We're very sorry to interrupt you, but. . ."

They both turned, saw us and smiled. "Hello," the man said. "We've got visitors!"

"Have you got your swimming cossies?" said the woman. "If you have, you're welcome to join us!"

I didn't know what to say to this, but afterwards Jenna said my face registered total

horror. "We're . . . er . . . looking for Mr Hugo,"
I said after a moment.

"Henry Hugo – that's me," said the man. He
pretended to look at his reflection in the patio
doors. "Or it was the last time I looked!"

"Oh, Henry!" said the woman. "You are a
scream."

"You're . . . Mr Hugo?" I asked. *Not dead after
all. . .*

He nodded and adjusted his bath hat slightly,
then indicated the woman in the plastic flowers.
"And this is my new lady wife. And who are you
two?"

"Well, we live in Bensbury," I began.

"Bensbury! Don't tell me the old trout sent
you?"

I shook my head, grinning. "No, she doesn't
know we're here. You see, the old . . . er . . . I
mean, Mrs Hugo employed me to do a bit of
work on the garden, and when I was digging
there I found this." I held up the newly-shiny
cigarette case. "I thought it might belong to you."

"Yes, that's mine all right – my initials are on
it," he said, grinning all over his face. "So the old
trout must have buried all my stuff!"

"What a way to carry on!" said the woman.

"But however did you find me?"

"Well, we thought you were abroad – that's what she tells people – and then we found out you weren't," I said, hoping he wasn't going to ask us how we found his address. "So we just thought we'd come over and give you this back."

"And I'm very pleased you did!" He got out of the tub – he was wearing a funny, old-fashioned striped swimming costume – and flung a towelling gown around his shoulders. He was small, just as Grouchy Green had said, and quite round and smiley. He wasn't a *bit* like Mrs Huge-o. He took the case, felt in one of the pockets of his towelling gown and pulled out a ten pound note. "Take this for your trouble, young chap, and if you find anything else of mine, there'll be more of these."

"I found a watch," I said, "but it was in pieces. I'm digging in your old garden quite regularly now, though, so I might easily find something else."

"And if you do, mum's the word, eh?"

"Mum's the word," I said. Whatever that meant.

We said goodbye and as we turned to go, the woman called, "I hear Bensbury's got a pageant on Saturday!"

Jenna nodded. "It's a special anniversary – they're re-enacting things that happened four hundred years ago. We had a witch living there then."

"You've got a witch living there now!" Mr Huge-o said, and we all laughed.

On the whole I was glad he wasn't dead.

CHAPTER NINE

"I thought I must be losing my psychic powers – I knew I couldn't feel anything spooky about Mr Huge-o," Jenna said on the bus back to Bensbury. "I don't know how you got the idea that he was dead and she'd killed him."

"I dunno either," I said. "I think I just liked the idea of her being arrested and carted away. I wouldn't have to go and dig her garden every week then."

We got off the bus on the other side of our village green. "They're still there, then!" Jenna said, pointing to the swarm of flies hovering in a dark cloud above the witch's hut.

As we grew closer, the fly-cloud wavered, dispersed, then re-formed again, a dark, ever-changing shape that looked as if it was coming closer. "I think we'll have to run for it," I said, and we raced across the green and got through our door just moments before the flies descended.

"Those blasted things!" Mum said as we charged into the shop. "Everyone's complaining about them. They're going to ruin the pageant if they hang around, you know."

"Can't they be sprayed or something?" I asked.

"Don't you think we've tried that? I've had every insecticide in the shop out there and those flies just seem to lap it up!"

Jenna and I walked through the shop into our back kitchen. "That's because they're not ordinary flies," she said to me in a low voice, "they're supernatural ones. They've materialized by means of some sort of spell."

"Some sort of spell cast by Mrs Witch?"

"I guess so."

"Then couldn't we do what they always do in *Buffy*?"

Jenna groaned.

"No, really! We ought to counteract one spell with another."

"Oh yeah – easy! And where are we going to find a spell like that?"

There was a moment's silence, then we both said it together: "*Witchfinding!*"

We got out the book and started going through it. It didn't actually have a list of spells to counteract other spells, but it did have a chapter called Country Wisdom and Traditions, giving the sorts of cures and medicines that would have been practised years ago by the local wise woman. These were for various ailments: cordials for coughs and colds, herbal mixtures for getting rid of freckles and sunburn, salves for cuts and nettle stings. At the end of all these there was a section with more the type of thing we wanted: nettle water to sprinkle around a house and rid it of fleas, a particular type of wood which, when burned, would smoke out rats – and a herbal mixture to get rid of flies.

Jenna read it out. "Tansy, mint, feverfew gathered at dusk and –" she gave a shriek – "powdered unicorn horn! Where are we supposed to get *that*?"

"Slightly difficult one, that. But we'll get as much of everything else as we can."

Jenna nodded. "Mum's got a book of wild flowers and herbs somewhere – we can use that to find the right ones." She read on and then said,

"But I think this mixture is more like a pot-pourri – the sort of thing you'd put in a room to scent it. I don't know how we're supposed to see off a whole swarm of flies with it."

"Well, maybe we'll have to mix it all up and chuck it in the air."

We sniggered a bit about this and then Jenna said, "But suppose by opposing her, Mrs Witch thinks we're throwing down some sort of challenge? Trying to fight her magic with our own? Suppose she comes back at us with something even worse?"

"I dunno," I said. "We'll just have to risk that."

There were eight herbs listed altogether and the next day we found five of them and dried them by putting them in the oven, turned on very low. They were supposed to dry naturally but that would have taken seven weeks and we didn't have the time, seeing as the pageant was only the following day. After they were dried, we crushed them up and put them in a bag, ready to throw at the flies. We were going to do this at dusk, because Jenna said it was the right time to do that sort of stuff – also the light was fading then and people wouldn't be able to see us.

The flies were hovering above the witch's hut when we came out, but they moved towards us in a blurry cloud almost immediately we closed the shop door. We ran off to the right of the green and when the swarm reached us, chucked handfuls of the herb mixture in the air, shouting, "Begone, flies!" because it sounded a bit olde worlde and a bit spell-like. But, yeah, it also sounded a bit daft.

We got about three handfuls in the air each and then Horseface Hall came out of her front door. "What are you two doing?" she said. "What's all that stuff you're throwing in the air?"

Obviously we couldn't begin to explain, so we didn't say anything.

"You want to be careful, messing about where those flies are!" she said, and then she went, "Oh! They're not there any more."

Jenna and I looked at each other, then straight up in the air and – well, we just couldn't believe it: the flies had *gone*. Completely vanished.

We went back indoors a bit stunned. Coincidence, or what?

We went to bed same time as usual, but for some reason I woke up just after midnight, feeling like

I'd had a full night's sleep already. I hauled myself on to the window seat and looked out of the window across the green. Everything looked OK out there: the bonfire and the witch's hut all ready, the stalls assembled. The witch's broom was outside the hovel, but there was no cat. Stuffer wasn't going to let them have the repaired Silky back before pageant day, just in case.

I looked down to the gravel path outside the shop, wondering what had woken me, and straight away saw the big black cat. It seemed to be waiting for something. . .

There was a noise from Jenna's bedroom. She'd woken up too, then. I heard her bedroom door click and thought that she'd come into my room.

She didn't, though, and the next thing I heard was her going downstairs, very softly. I thought she might be going to get a drink, so I waited for her to come up, but instead heard the bolts on the shop door being pulled back. When I looked out of the window she was there, standing next to the cat. This was really odd: not only that she should suddenly get the urge to go outside in the middle of the night, but that she'd go without telling me.

I pulled the window up. "Hey!" I said in a loud whisper. "What're you doing?"

She made no response at all.

"Jenna!" I hissed.

Nothing.

Well, what could I do? I quickly found my hoodie, pulled it on over my pyjamas and went downstairs. She'd left the shop door wide open, so I made it look as if it was closed without actually closing it, and went off after her. She was a little way away, heading around the green.

"Jenna!" I hissed. "Where're you going?" She didn't turn or react in any way – and then it came to me. Of course! She was *sleepwalking*. And wasn't it dangerous to wake sleepwalkers?

Instead, I joined the queue. First was the cat, stalking along with its tail in the air, then Jenna in a long white nightie, then me, hunched into my hoodie and wondering what the blooming heck was going on.

Before too long I realized Jenna was talking to herself, making little noises of distress: cries and whimpers. A couple of times she actually called out like she was in pain, and rubbed at one of her limbs, and when she did this I felt a sharp pain down my own arm or in my leg, and knew that I was feeling this through her.

I was worried that the cat was going to lead us

over towards the witch's hut and Jenna would disappear into it and never be seen again, but it didn't, it just stalked around the green, following the outside path. It took about ten minutes to do the full circuit and get back to the shop, and by this time Jenna was whimpering all the time, so much so that I was really getting spooked.

We passed the shop, the black cat still leading the way, and started on what would be our second circuit. I decided then that I'd have to wake her or we might end up walking round in circles for the rest of the night. I overtook and stood a way in front of her, then clapped my hands and waved as she approached. She just didn't seem to see me, though, so I grabbed both her hands and said, "Jenna! Jenna, wake up!"

She did the whimpering thing again, and shivered as if she was freezing cold, so (real gentlemanly, this) I took off my hoodie and put it around her, then shook her shoulders. "Wakey, wakey!" I said.

"Oh!" A tremor ran through her body, she looked at me in shock, and then seemed to come to herself. She started crying – full-on, not the usual carry-on she does when she wants Mum to take her side. I pulled her back towards the shop (the cat, by the way, had completely disappeared), we went in and I sat her down on the chair the oldies use.

"Sssh," I said. "You're crying really loudly. You'll wake Mum!"

"It was awful . . . awful!" she sobbed.

"What was?"

"Hateful and horrible!"

I took a kitchen roll off the shelf, opened it and passed her a couple of pieces of paper. "*What was?*"

She blew her nose and looked at me bleakly. "They dragged her round the green! Round and round on a trestle thing at the back of a cart. Her head bumped against stones and her arms and legs got scraped and scratched so that she was bleeding all over. Not only that, but they threw stones at her. She lost consciousness after she'd been round once, and she had five more rounds still to go."

I gawped at her. "Are you talking about Old Ma Morgan?"

She nodded. "In my dream, I was her."

"Blimey," I said.

"She made me see what it was like." She started crying again. "I think she truly was a witch – but even so, no one deserves that sort of treatment."

"They don't," I agreed.

"I mean, they were just *vicious* to her." She shuddered. "While I was walking round, I was feeling what she was feeling – every stone, every bump and graze and cut."

I didn't say anything, but what I was thinking was I was glad it wasn't *me* who was the psychic one.

"I think ... I get the feeling that Old Ma Morgan intends to take her revenge on the village for what she suffered. And I think she might do it on the night of the pageant."

"So what shall we do?" I asked, alarmed.

"That's just it," Jenna said. "I don't know what we *can* do. For a start, who's going to believe us?"

I stared at her, knowing she was right, and then I looked at my watch and a shiver ran over me. Just eighteen hours to go. . .

CHAPTER TEN

I could have done with a bit of a lie-in the next morning because I hadn't recovered from trailing Jenna around half the night, but there was no chance of this because Mum wanted us up early; said she was expecting it to be her busiest day ever. While she was opening up the shop and I was stuffing down cereal and toast, Jenna went to get *Witchfinding*.

She thumbed through the pages a bit and then stopped and gave a little scream. "I knew it!" she said.

"Whooa?" (My mouth was full.)

"Listen," she said, and read out: "*Before sentence was carried out on Old Ma Morgan, she was further punished. A rough trailer being*

constructed from rushes and willow, the said
witch was lashed to this by her arm and leg,
and the trailer attached to the back of a farm
cart. It made six circuits of the green, and the
village people, being encouraged to vent their
anger upon her, threw all manner of rotten
vegetables and fruit, also stones and rubble, at
the witch."

I pulled a face. "What happened then?"

"The witch, being dragged to the place of
execution, was tied firmly to a stake in the centre
of a commodious bonfire and asked to repent.
She did not, but instead called out in a strong
voice that she was innocent of all crimes. If she
had any power, however, she said she would use
it to curse the village for carrying out such an
abominable act on a harmless old woman. . ."

"So," I said thoughtfully, "was she saying she
was a real witch, with genuine powers, or not?"

Jenna looked at me, troubled. "I guess we
might find that out tonight."

"Twins!" Mum called from the shop. "Can one
of you come and serve, please! There are already
three people waiting."

I went, because I was still a bit peckish and
fancied a new variety of crisps in a very large

packet. Also, I'd had a quick look to see who was waiting to be served. . .

"Good morning, Mrs Hugo," I said smarmily, moving forward to take her shopping list. "I'm afraid I won't be over to dig the garden today because Mum needs us both in the shop."

She sniffed. "Well, for all the progress you're making, I don't suppose it'll make much difference."

I looked down at her list, went to get washing-up liquid and soap powder, then hesitated over the packet of rice. "Do you want Italian or Indian rice?" I asked. "Oh – *Italy*. Didn't you say that that's where Mr Hugo was?"

She frowned at me fatly. "I didn't say where he was."

"Oh! My mistake. Thought you did. Perhaps you said somewhere different – somewhere else where the water's warm. . ."

There was a choking noise from Jenna, who'd come along to see what I was up to. Mrs Huge-o frowned, obviously not getting it.

We stared each other out for a moment and then she said stonily, "Whilst I'm here, I might as well tell you that your digging is *not* up to standard."

"Oh?"

"And it looks to me as if you've been digging my garden *just* where I said you shouldn't."

"Well," I said slowly, looking at her with my head on one side, "it's just *some* parts of your garden are a lot more interesting than other parts. If you know what I mean. . ."

Her fat cheeks quivered. She knew what I was getting at all right. "That's as maybe," she snapped, "but if you can't follow my directives then I'm afraid I shall have to terminate your employment."

A big grin spread all over my face. "Way to go!" I said cheerfully. I rubbed my hands together. "I'll go and get your Italian rice then, shall I?"

As the afternoon went on, more and more people arrived for the pageant and by the evening there were cars and coaches from neighbouring villages parked all round the green. It grew dark and flaming torches were lit and stuck into the ground and candle-lanterns hung on to the stalls. It looked really good, actually, especially as the crinklies behind the stalls were wearing what was supposed to be seventeenth-century gear: smocks and baggy, old-fashioned skirts and trousers, with hooded cloaks over the top.

When the play began – well, it wasn't exactly the Royal Shakespeare Company, but it was kind of OK. The first part of it went well, the actors and actresses playing the olde tyme villagers acted out their ailments, then went to visit the hovel of Old Ma Morgan (played by Bumface Butley, for all she was worth) to get their cures. After that there was a break for what Ratty called "village jollities" and people started spending their money at the stalls: rolling a penny, bowling for a piglet, apple-bobbing, and so on.

I met up with Jenna, who was pretending to be a beautiful village maiden. "Everything OK?" I asked, because she was looking a bit spooked. She was doing the main part of her role – when she would pretend to light the bonfire with Old Ma Morgan on it – during the second half of the play.

She nodded and gave a shiver. "I've been looking for Mrs Witch, but there's no sign of her. She's here somewhere, though, and something's going to happen. I can *feel* it."

I nodded. "We'll just have to try and be ready, then."

"Come along, you two!" Slurry Murray, who was on the apple-bobbing stall, shouted to us. "You're young. You show the others how to do it!"

I groaned, but Jenna pulled my sleeve. (My *orange* sleeve; I was already wearing my firebrand outfit. And yeah, the T-shirt, not the nightie.) "Oh, come on," she said. "It's only for a laugh."

"You mean more of a laugh than being a firebrand?" I asked. "Is that really possible?"

We went over to the big old barrel filled with water. It had had ten or so green apples bobbing about on it and the object was to get hold of one between your teeth and lift it out. I watched Jenna for a while, seeing if she could do it (she couldn't) then bent down to show her how. As I put my face in the cold water and opened my mouth ready to take a bite from the nearest apple, Jenna, who was still trying, gave a gurgled scream. "Toads!" she shrieked.

I jerked out my head immediately and saw to my horror that, instead of apples bobbing about, there were now toads in the barrel: horrible, dark green and slimy, their flat, ugly heads above the water, their bulbous eyes protruding. Toads – and I'd nearly bitten one! I gave a roar of disgust, and so did Jenna. She was shuddering with revulsion; I was almost sick.

"What the blooming. . .?" Slurry Murray said, looking at the barrel in disbelief. "I don't believe it! However could. . .?" He bent right over the barrel, peering at the toads through his glasses. "I've never seen anything like this in my life!"

I took a deep breath and steeled myself to look into the barrel again, but in that instant everything changed. The toads vanished and the green apples came back.

"Did you see that?" Slurry addressed the world in general. "I've never seen anything so peculiar!"

"What's that, Mr Murray?" asked Mrs (Piggy) Pinder, who happened to be passing.

"Well, you won't believe this, but just now those apples were toads!" said the old chap, flabbergasted.

She gave a short, pig-like squeal. "You're right, I *don't* believe it," she said, while Jenna and I just stood there with soaking wet faces, feeling utterly sickened. Were the toads part of Old Ma Morgan's revenge?

"It's true as I stand here!" said Slurry.

"I think you've been on the scrumpy," she snorted.

"You two saw 'em, didn't you?" Slurry asked us. "Sure you did. That's why you got your heads out so quick."

"And I saw them, also," a voice said, and Jenna and I both turned and nearly jumped out of our skins to find Mrs Witch standing behind us. "Toads are strange reptiles," she said quietly. "They're a witch's familiars. Did you know that?"

"Course we did!" I said, and I grabbed Jenna's arm and pulled her away.

"Why did you do that?" Jenna said when we'd got some distance away. "We should have stayed and faced her out."

"Survival instinct," I said. "What chance d'you think *we've* got against a witch as powerful as she must be?"

Jenna looked through the crowd towards her. "No chance, I don't suppose. . ."

Ratty rang the bell to signal the start of the second half of the play and I groaned. Jenna was quite looking forward to her big part, but I certainly wasn't. Not at all. I didn't know *how* I'd ended up as a dancing firebrand.

The audience gathered again in groups around where the action was to be, and the play restarted with the constables coming to the witch's house and accusing her of witchcraft. There was a short trial scene, then the judge read the sentence:

"The said witch is to be trussed on to a cart and pulled around the village green six times so that her neighbours can have their revenge on her wrong-doings. And then she will be burned at the stake until she is nought but ashes."

The whole audience fell silent at this and it was all quite eerie. Horrible. Especially when you knew that Old Ma Morgan – whether she had been a real witch or not – *had* been put to death.

I was in the shadows just out of view of the audience as the next scene began and Jenna stepped forward to tie "Old Ma Morgan" on to the stake in the centre of the bonfire.

"Way to go, sis," I whispered under my breath. Jenna said her lines and had just moved into a gap in the bonfire holding a rope when I realized that someone was standing beside me: *Mrs Witch*.

Jenna turned away from the audience and looked towards me. "Jake," she hissed. "I know something bad's going to happen. Be careful."

I didn't have time to answer before she went on with her speech, saying how she would tie the knots tightly and that the wickedness of the witch would be consumed by flames. When I looked at what she was doing, though, she wasn't tying the witch to the stake at all, but just leaving the ropes hanging loose. She said to me later that she'd just known that she should leave them untied.

She stepped back from the bonfire and was handed the white taper she was supposed to light the fire with.

I was on. As she bent down to pretend to light the fire, the firebrand was supposed to go into action. I leapt forward with a shout and a jump, but suddenly, mystifyingly, the bonfire erupted in a *whoosh* of flame, just as it had done in the vision we'd both had. This time, though, it was for real.

There was a collective scream from the audience, I leapt backwards and away and, before anyone else could do anything, Mrs Witch ran forward. She pulled Jenna to one side, out of the way of the flames, then shouted at Bumface Butley to jump down from the box she was standing on, *quickly*! Luckily, Bumface not being tied up, she could do this straight away, and Mrs Witch helped her down and rolled her on the ground to put out the few little flames around the edge of her skirt.

Everyone was screaming and yelling by this time, and of course Mum ran up and started making a huge fuss, but when it was clear that everyone was OK, they let the bonfire go on burning. As it blazed, Jenna said they should put all the flimsy wood of the witch's house on the bonfire, too, so that every last trace of Old Ma Morgan would be gone from the village. Stuffer and Mr Tragic did this, and in the confusion no one thought to ask who'd actually instructed that it should be done. The rest of the evening – well, the only other interesting thing to happen was seeing the big black cat walking slowly across the green and disappearing into the distance.

"Sorry," I said to Mrs Witch the following morning in our kitchen, "but as you weren't very friendly, we thought you were the reincarnation of the witch, come back to take your revenge on the village."

She laughed. She looked quite normal (well, NFB) when she did this. "Really," she said. "There aren't such things as witches!"

Neither Jenna nor I replied to this.

"But I can quite see why you thought I was unfriendly," she went on, "because people do tend to think I'm a bit stand-offish. I'm not really, though, I'm rather shy," she added, going red as she said this last bit.

"So," Jenna said, "it was just a lucky coincidence that you happened to be standing near us."

Mrs Witch nodded. "I came over to watch the pageant, and afterwards I was going to ask you both to tea." She looked a bit embarrassed. "It was nice of you to come round with the vicar and welcome me to the village, and I felt I'd been a bit short with you."

"Oh, right," Jenna said, while I squirmed a bit, thinking that it was lucky she didn't know what we'd really come round for.

"And I felt worse when I discovered that the black cat really *had* been in my house that time."

"I thought I'd seen him!" I said.

The three of us were quiet for a moment, then Jenna said, "So what do we really think happened last night, then?"

"Well, I've done a bit of dabbling in ancient lore," said Mrs Witch, "and though I don't believe in witches, I do believe that sometimes things happen that just can't be explained."

"Like the toads?"

"Yes, like the toads," she said. "The power of suggestion is a very strong one."

"And d'you think it's possible that Old Ma Morgan's spirit was somehow called back to earth by the activity surrounding the anniversary of her death?" I asked.

"Because that's what we think," Jenna added.

Mrs Witch shook her head. "I think that might be taking things a little bit too far."

"So how do you explain the bonfire igniting?" Jenna asked, just as Mum came in from the shop.

"Yes, that was a strange thing, wasn't it?" Mum said. "A fork of lightning at the very moment Jenna was pretending to light the bonfire!"

Jenna and I exchanged glances. This was the conclusion that everyone at the pageant had come to: that a rogue fork of lightning had somehow caused the bonfire to catch.

"*Very* odd," Mum went on. "Lightning with no thunder or rain! It made an excellent finale to the evening, though, once everyone had got over the shock."

Mrs Witch stood up. "I must be off," she said. "All my bits and pieces are arriving in a removal van today and I want to be ready for them."

"Oh, I thought you'd already moved in, Mrs Wychwood," said Mum.

"I have," she said, "but most of my things have been in storage. Now I can fill up the shelves and mantelpieces and make Meadow Cottage look a bit more homely."

Jenna and I looked at each other. Mrs Witch was all right, really – and of course, wasn't a witch at all. We'd have to think of another name for her.

As we went through to the shop, three women came in together, all nattering excitedly. Mum looked at them with surprise, because on Sundays we only opened to sell newspapers. "Good morning, Mrs Scudder, Miss Hall and Mrs Murray!" she called. "What can I do for you?"

"We'd like the Lost Puss notices taken down," Scatty Scudder said.

"Because our cats have all come back!" said Horseface Hall.

"Really?" Mum marvelled.

Mrs Slurry Murray nodded. "They came walking up the road together as right as ninepence! Nothing wrong with them at all!"

I clapped my hands. "Yay!" I said. "They'd been on a cats' night out."

Jenna leant towards me. "When the witch's cat's away. . ." she whispered.

". . .the village cats can play," I finished.

As Mrs Witch went off with the other women, Jenna and I returned to the kitchen with a couple of choccy bars to keep us going until lunchtime.

"So – another ghostly incident solved," she said. "We'd just better make sure that they don't have any more witch-burning pageants around here."

I nodded agreement. "We just about got away with it this time."

"I mean, there are enough everyday ghosts in Bensbury without calling up witches from four hundred years ago."

"Especially – as her dear departed husband said – when we've already got Mrs Huge-o. . ."

Look out for more seriously spooky
adventures...

HAUNTED HOUSE

When Jake and Jenna move to a village in the middle of nowhere Jake's sure that years of boredom stretch ahead of them. Until Jenna sees the ghost...

From then on Jake and Jenna decide that ghost-hunting will be the new hobby that Mum's always on at them about. Who'd have thought that such a small place could have so many? There's the wandering ghost dog and – much more spooky – the restless spirit that haunts the tumbledown empty house, weeping and wailing. No one knows why it's so sad, but Jake and Jenna are determined to find out – even if it means staying up all night in the dark, deserted, very *haunted* house...

PLAGUE HOUSE

When Jake and Jenna stumble across
Corpses' Copse one day, they know
there's something very sinister about it.
Jenna hears children singing "Ring a
Ring o' Roses", the chilling nursery
rhyme that dates from the time of the
Plague... The villagers warn the twins to
keep away from the copse, but Jenna is
sure that a ghost from the past
desperately needs her help, and she *can't*
say no...

HORROR HOUSE

"Feel how cold my fingers are!"

"Wow!" I said, for her hands were polar-bear cold and, when she touched me, the coldness seemed to move through me like frost.

As I began shivering I realized that the front door was open slightly and only a few steps away, so I shoved Jenna through it and stumbled after her. Another second and we were both standing outside on the step, blinking in the sunshine.

We took some deep breaths, and Jenna spread her arms wide and turned her face up to the sun. "That was horrible," she said.

"But what actually *was* it?" I asked. "What happened?"

She shook her head. "I don't know," she said slowly, "but it's not just this damp business. Something's wrong in Horror House. Something's *very* wrong. . ."